UNIPIGGLE
The Unicorn Pig!

Dragon Trouble

HANNAH SHAW

USBORNE

Twinkleland Palace

Better Land

The Harbour

Twinkletown

Village of Fancy Pants

Bug Island

Dragonton Cave Complex

Volcano Lake

Twinkleland

(And surrounding kingdoms)

The Tree place

Twinklesea
(Underwater Kingdom)

Bright Point

Twee-on-Sea

Little Charming

The Fairy well dell
(To Rabbitland)

Pigs Ear

The Farm

Rainbow falls

The Wild bit

To other Land

This is Princess Peony Peachykins Primrose
Pollyanna Posh, usually known as Princess Pea.
She lives in Twinkleland Palace with her parents,
Queen Bee and King Barry.

She likes: mud, marshmallows, chocolate and
having fun.

TWINKLELAND!

This is Unipiggle. He's Princess Pea's new Royal Companion. He's a loud, muddy and proud unicorn pig.

He likes: mud, marshmallows, chocolate, having fun and getting tickled behind the ears.

Princess Pea was supposed to choose a **UNICORN** as her Royal Companion. But during the Unicorn Parade, there was a **STORM** and things went a bit **WRONG**. Luckily, Unipiggle saved the Princess and the day.

Now Princess Pea and Unipiggle are the best of friends and can't wait to go on lots of adventures together.

(It's a good thing the Princess didn't end up with a *typical* unicorn, because they are vain and snooty and have fussy grooms.)

Dashing Dancer wants sparkly hooves today and cucumber to cool his eyes!

Palace Pranks

Everything was as it should be in Twinkleland Royal Palace.

Well, *almost.*

The Palace Pixies were busy keeping the hundreds of rooms and turrets sparkling clean and extremely tidy.

King Barry was trying out some trendy new moustache styles with a new set of curling tongs.

How do I look?

Queen Bee was in the Royal Kitchens
organizing the lunch menu with the Chef Pixie.

But was their only daughter, Princess Pea, having her early morning tapestry lesson in the sewing room as planned?

No, she was NOT.

In fact, Princess Pea was throwing
apples from her secret treehouse!
And in the Royal Orchard below,
Unipiggle was ready and waiting...

"Oink!"

The unicorn pig zapped the apple in mid-air with his magical rainbow horn, instantly turning it into…**CHOCOLATE**.

Zaaappp!

"Gobble, gobble! Yum!" He wolfed it down noisily.

Unipiggle had a special kind of magic:
he could turn objects into chocolate. Apples,
lettuce, puddles, crowns, slippers, loo seats…
This had been causing lots of trouble around
Twinkleland Palace. The disgruntled Palace
Pixies had been finding sticky chocolate marks
in the most unlikely places…

Not everyone in
Twinkleland had magic,
but those who did
weren't allowed to
use it because
that was against
the **RULES**.

After some magic-related mishaps, Queen Bee and King Barry had decided it was just too messy and unpredictable for everyday use. (But Unipiggle didn't pay any attention to **RULES**.)

The Queen liked everything to be **100% PERFECT** and making **RULES** was her favourite pastime.

✦ TOP RULES ✦

Be perfect

There must be no grubbiness

Be neatly completely

Politeness at all times

Check: Are you smiling cheerfully?

No laziness or dawdling

Important: Do NOT use magic*
* except in a big and terrible emergency

One of the Royal Rules stated that Princess Pea wasn't allowed to go past the palace gates on her own. Princess Pea wasn't entirely sure if this was to keep her out of trouble or to make sure that *she* didn't cause trouble elsewhere. The King was happy to let the Queen make all the rules because his favourite pastimes were moustache-grooming and composing terrible songs on his ukulele, and so far there weren't any rules against those.

Back in the treehouse, Princess Pea slid down her super-slidey pole and joined Unipiggle on the ground to munch on a chocolate apple. The Princess wasn't allowed sweets, but since Unipiggle had arrived, she'd realized she could have chocolate whenever she liked as long as her parents didn't find out! (Although she always made sure to brush her teeth twice a day.)

She looked around the orchard. "Humph. I'm bored of throwing apples. What shall we do instead?"

Peering over the orchard hedge, Princess Pea and Unipiggle scanned the Third Best Palace Garden for mischievous ideas. The Princess spotted an empty flower bed ready to be planted with spring bulbs and grinned. "How about we make some muddy puddles?"

"Grunt!" Unipiggle agreed with a cheeky grin.

Puddles were rare in the palace gardens (the weather was usually too perfect) so they had to make their own.

After tiring themselves out, the mud-splattered Princess sat down on a large toadstool and Unipiggle flopped down next to her. They stared longingly at the view. Twinkleland Palace was high on a hill and the rest of the Magical Kingdom of Twinkleland shimmered invitingly below. Princess Pea remembered her parents had promised that when she got her Royal Unicorn, she would be allowed to go for rides outside the palace...

Well, she was ready and so was Unipiggle!

Princess Pea ran back to her treehouse, leaving Unipiggle trying to scratch his muddy behind on a polished golden statue. She rummaged through a suitcase full of old books she'd discovered a while ago in a forgotten turret, and picked out the one she was looking for.

Returning with an old leather-bound journal, the Princess waved it under Unipiggle's snout.

"Listen, Unipiggle, we need to have an **ADVENTURE**... And this book is going to give us some great ideas!"

Unipiggle sniffed the journal curiously.

Princess Pea opened it to a tattered page and began to read out loud.

SIR Sneeze-A-lot

I bade my farewell to the dragons in Dragonton caves and made my way through wild and steaming jungles on the slopes of the dormant volcano. I was told I would discover a magical volcanic lake in the crater at the top, surrounded by boggy swamps. Legend has it that the lake can grant any wish you desire. Unfortunately, on the way I caught a bad case of the sniffles! Alas, I had to change my plans and take a different path to reach Fancy Pants Village before nightfall.

ADVENTURES IN TWINKLELAND

Dragons! A boggy swamp! A wild jungle!
And a magical lake that granted wishes! These
things seemed thrilling to Princess Pea.

"It's time to go somewhere really *exciting* and
really **MUDDY**, Unipiggle!" she cried. "We need
to get out of the palace, find these places and
EXPLORE TWINKLELAND!"

Unipiggle grunted happily, especially at the
boggy swamp idea. He rolled over and wiggled
his filthy trotters in the air.

Princess Pea grinned. It was **ADVENTURE
TIME** with Unipiggle!

Green Porridge

The bell for elevenses rang, but Princess Pea and Unipiggle pretended not to hear it, as they were too busy planning their adventures.

They only rushed inside when they saw Queen Bee strolling determinedly through the palace gardens, looking for them (and discovering the flower bed full of muddy holes).

Without stopping to wipe their feet and trotters, Princess Pea and Unipiggle ran in through the palace's back door. Unipiggle skidded down the perfectly polished marble corridors behind the Princess, towards the Grand Hall.

Princess Pea dashed to her throne and sat down at the table seconds before her mummy came marching back in. Unipiggle had dived onto a plush velvet sofa in the corner and was pretending to be asleep. The King hadn't even noticed their arrival because he'd got watercress porridge stuck in his beard and was trying to comb it out.

"There you are!" said Queen Bee to Princess Pea. "Do you know why there are MUDDY PUDDLES in the garden, darling?"

Unipiggle attempted a fake snore but instead let out a noisy parp.

Parp!

Princess Pea tried to rub her muddy hands clean on her muddy dungarees, but only succeeded in making them muddier.

"No idea, Mummy!"

Toot! Toot!

Elevenses for Queen Brunella Beatrix and Princess Peony Peachykins are served.

"Oh, delicious," lied Princess Pea. "GREEN porridge!" She secretly hoped Unipiggle might turn her porridge into chocolate. It wasn't that the Princess didn't *like* the green and healthy food that was served for every meal, but it got a bit boring eating the same things all the time.

"So…" The Queen peered intently at Princess Pea. "If you haven't been making muddy puddles, what *have* you been doing?"

"Oh, I've been reading, Mummy!" said the Princess, not lying this time.

"Have you?" asked the King. "Bravo!"

"Very good. A perfect Princess activity!" agreed the Queen, in a surprised voice. Unipiggle jumped off his sofa and galloped over to Princess Pea.

The Princess winked at Unipiggle.
"Yes, I'm reading a very interesting book
about Twinkleland."
She didn't want to alarm
her parents, so she
put some of the
slimy watercress
porridge in
her mouth.

SLURP SLURP

"I wondered if you knew
where I could find some old
maps ***SLURP*** so I can, erm...look up
something."

King Barry's moustache began to waggle.
He loved old maps! Putting his elbow in his

porridge, he began to tell Princess Pea that Twinkletown Library was full of old maps and interesting books. "The library has all of *our* old books and maps actually," the Queen chimed in. "They were far too dusty to keep here in the palace, so I kindly donated them for everyone to enjoy."

Princess Pea had never visited the library before, but she knew Twinkletown was only a

stone's throw from the palace. (Not that anyone EVER threw stones in Twinkleland — they didn't even skim pebbles for fun.)

"Could I please visit the library today, Mummy and Daddy?" Princess Pea asked as sweetly as she could.

Unipiggle held his breath…

The Queen smiled. "How very studious of you! I shall cancel your other lessons. I can't take you, I'm afraid, as I have lots of important rotas to organize in the palace."

"I'm tuning my ukulele today, peasprout," apologized the King.

"I could ask a pixie to come with me?" the Princess suggested hopefully.

"Very well," said the Queen. "But make sure

you are polite at all times. Here, take some carrot sticks and apple slices for lunch."

She looked sternly at Unipiggle. "And remember, *no* magic…or chocolate."

Unipiggle grinned and tried to give the impression he'd never been in any trouble, ever.

Princess Pea was pleased. The first part of
their plan was coming together very nicely!
She patted Unipiggle fondly. "We'll be perfectly
behaved…"

Ready for Adventure

Princess Pea knew exactly which pixie
to take with her on this adventure.
She found Arthur the Gardener Pixie
in the First Best Palace Garden.

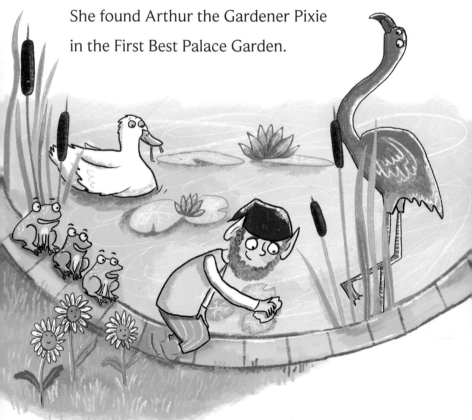

"Good morning, Arthur!" sang the Princess cheerfully.

Arthur jumped out of his skin, lost his balance and fell into the pond. The frogs stopped croaking and started laughing and the daisies in the grass laughed too — tiny, shrill little squeals.

OINK!

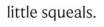

Princess Pea helped Arthur out of the water. "Oops! You're a bit soggy to go on an adventure with us now."

"Go on an *adventure*?" repeated Arthur nervously, emptying water from his hat. "I can't do that. What would the Queen say?" Arthur's job was to maintain the enormous palace gardens to an exceptionally high standard, which meant he never ever stopped working.

"Unipiggle and I have been given permission to leave the palace," Princess Pea reassured him. "And I've chosen you to come with us...because I like you!"

Arthur couldn't help feeling flattered. "But where are we going?"

"The library," declared Princess Pea. "Well, at least that's where we're going first. We need to find a map to plan the *rest* of our adventure."

Arthur the gardener breathed a huge sigh of relief. "The Queen wants me to accompany you to Twinkletown Library?"

"Yes." The Princess smiled. "Go and get ready!"

It was almost noon. Princess Pea and Unipiggle were waiting by the huge palace gates, feeling very excited. The Princess was already wearing her royal cape and her trusty wellies, and she was carrying her hastily-packed satchel. In it was a rope, a freshly-sharpened pencil, a notebook, *Adventures in Twinkleland* and the apple slices and carrot sticks.

Unipiggle hadn't packed anything — he was always prepared.

Chug-a-chug-a-chug! Arthur appeared on the only vehicle he owned: the Palace Lawnmower.

"Lead on, Princess Pea and Royal Piggy!" he declared, revving his lawnmower like it was a sports car.

Princess Pea smothered a giggle and then leaped onto Unipiggle's back. *"Giddy up, Unipiggle!"*

Unipiggle responded by rearing up into the air and squealing happily.

Princess Pea breathed deeply as the Gate Pixie pushed open the golden gates.

"Do you smell that?" she asked her companions, as Unipiggle trotted over the

moat-bridge and down the
hill towards Twinkletown.

"Is it Unipiggle parping again?"
called Arthur over the noise of his mower.

"No, silly. It's the whiff of freedom
and a brand-new adventure!" sighed
Princess Pea happily.

They were on their way!

Twinkletown Library

The Princess had only been to Twinkletown on the rare occasions when the Queen had taken her shopping for pairs of silly, pointy shoes (that she never wore).

Twinkletown had won the **Tidiest Town in Twinkleland Kingdom** competition every year and Princess Pea now began to see why. The quaint candy-coloured houses gleamed like they had been freshly painted that morning (which they probably had). The glass windows were so clean that they dazzled passers-by…

"*Whee! Whee!*" Unipiggle's trotters slippe
on the highly polished cobblestones. Princess
Pea clung on tight as Unipiggle skidded down
the street, with Arthur struggling to keep up on
his lawnmower.

The town square was adorned with colourful bunting and bluebirds glided elegantly overhead. Could Twinkletown be any more ***perfect***?

Oh, please mind the spray, Princess!

Unipiggle's snout twitched as they passed the bakery. The Baker Troll was icing a towering five-tier cake. It was the most stunning cake

rincess Pea had ever seen! Then she noticed
the window display was full of cakes just like it.
The baker rushed out with a slice of cake each for
the Princess and Arthur and a bun for Unipiggle.

It's all sugar-free!
I trust you'll inform
the Queen that none
of my cakes will harm
your teeth.

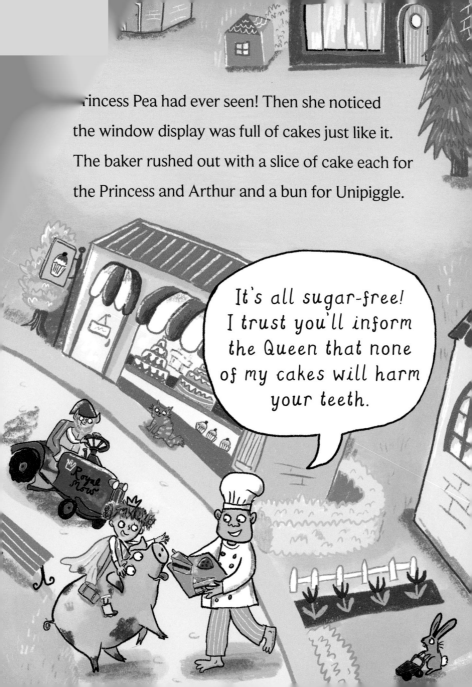

"Er, thank you!" said Princess Pea graciously, but the baker had already rushed back to his work.

"Ah, here we are," said Arthur, as they crossed Twinkletown Square. "This is where I get all my gardening books." He parked his mower and jumped off.

Princess Pea dismounted from Unipiggle and read the notice on the door.

LIBRARY

No Loud Noises
No Flying
No Running
No Muddy Feet
No Food or Drink
No Pets

"It doesn't say *No Royal Companions*," said Princess Pea, so Unipiggle barged open the heavy door. It did not creak as you might imagine, because hinges were kept well-oiled at all times in Twinkleland.

Twinkletown Library was awe-inspiring, crammed with colourful books that ran from floor to ceiling!

Ooh, it's wonderful!

LIBRARY Quiet Please!

RETURNS

shhhhhh!

51

"SHHH! This is a L.I.B.R.A.R.Y. You always whisper in a LIBRARY," wheezed a wizened old wizard, who was sitting at a desk, stamping books.

"No pets allowed," the wizard continued, looking over his glasses and frowning at Unipiggle.

Unipiggle glared back.

"Oh, he isn't just a **NORMAL** pet pig," Princess Pea said clearly. "He is my friend and my **Royal Companion**, Unipiggle."

The wizard blinked. He hadn't been expecting *royal* visitors.

"Have you got any old map books, please?" the Princess asked in her best, most polite voice.

The wizard softened and smiled. "Of course, Princess. I think there is a map book on the red or orange shelf. I would use magic to get it down, *ho ho*, but that would be cheating, of course!"

So Princess Pea climbed up a tall ladder to look at the red and orange books, while Arthur got distracted by a seed catalogue and Unipiggle had a power-nap on a beanbag in the corner.

Princess Pea climbed back down the ladder with a large book and opened it up on a table.

She rummaged through her satchel, took out *Adventures in Twinkleland* and turned to the page she'd earmarked.

After a few minutes of carefully peering at the map, the Princess found what she thought could be the location of Sir Sneeze-A-Lot's magical lake in an old volcano. She took out a pencil and notebook from her bag and made a copy of the map.

"Look, Arthur. This is where I want to go. There's a magical lake and a lovely swamp!" The Princess thought it was best not to mention it would be **BOGGY** and **MUDDY** because she didn't want to put Arthur off.

"That's only a few Twinklemiles south," Arthur whispered. "But...surely...are we allowed—"

"Good!" interrupted Princess Pea, as she nudged Unipiggle awake. "Because that's where we're heading next!"

5

Weeds and Wildness

The wizard had been so busy stamping books that he didn't see the polite Princess, the unusual pig and the pixie slip out of the door. (Much later he would end up stepping in some *Unipiggy* poop which had been accidentally left on the front step, but that would be the least of his worries by then.)

Unipiggle had glanced at the hand-drawn map and seemed confident about where they were going, so he was leading the way. Princess Pea was on his back, while Arthur trundled along on his mower.

Manely Tails
Unicorn Salon

They passed a unicorn
grooming salon, and heard the sound of
hairdryers. Unipiggle grunted disapprovingly as
a beautiful turquoise unicorn stepped out of the
stable door, arrogantly flicking his glossy mane.
The unicorn snorted rudely when he saw
Unipiggle but Unipiggle
didn't care.

He was the Royal
Unicorn now and
that meant he
was the best!

The road took them out of Twinkletown. The verges were freshly mown and white picket fences surrounded fields of perfect pumpkins growing plumply in straight lines. Even the tractor they saw was sparkling clean. The farmers in Twinkleland were very proud.

This wouldn't have been quite so bad if there hadn't been lots and lots of road signs bossing them around all the time:

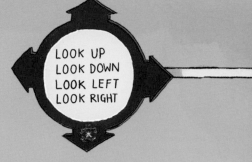

LOOK UP
LOOK DOWN
LOOK LEFT
LOOK RIGHT

"I don't know which way to look!" complained Princess Pea to Unipiggle. "It's all the same boring stuff here anyway. Where is the wild, magical land written about in Sir Sneeze-A-Lot's journal? I can't wait to get to a place where we can have a proper adventure and get really **MUDDY**!"

"Muddy?" asked Arthur, looking increasingly worried.

All of a sudden, he slammed the brakes on his mower.

"What is it?" cried the Princess with alarm.

Arthur was staring at the road. "There's a...a...a...**leaf**!!!!"

61

Unipiggle oinked a little laugh and Princess Pea rolled her eyes. "And?" she asked.

"Well, leaves don't belong in roads. They should be strictly ON trees," Arthur said firmly. "And weeds should strictly NOT be anywhere," he spluttered disbelievingly, pointing out a single dandelion.

But I'm bee friendly!

They turned a bend in the road and all of a sudden the landscape changed completely. No longer was everything in perfectly straight lines. Ahead, a rocky outcrop of hills was covered with a sprawling forest, and huge boulders were fringed by long grasses. A gentle breeze blew the scent of sweeties and forest fruits towards them. They could just hear the distant sounds of tropical birds playing trombones and insects buzzing in rhythm.

"Finally!" The Princess smiled. "It's getting **wilder**!"

Unipiggle grunted happily.

Princess Pea got down and walked next to Unipiggle for a while, enjoying the sensation of uneven ground beneath her feet. They passed a scrumptious marshmallow tree and the Princess carefully picked a few fluffy ones to share. This was a hopeful place. It felt like *anything* could happen.

Unfortunately, anything *did* happen, and it happened next.

"P-P-Princess?" stammered Arthur, stopping the mower again.

"Have you spotted another dandelion?" joked Princess Pea, popping the last morsel of her marshmallow into her mouth.

"No…noo. Oh me, oh my!"

Princess Pea looked…

Unipiggle looked…

(Yes, look, just **LOOK AT THAT!**)

There, ahead, a **monstrous beast** was eating a tree.

6 Dragon Trouble

The Princess blinked.

Unipiggle burped. (Oops.)

"Is it a dragon?" cried Arthur.

Princess Pea knew what dragons looked like.

She had a book called *The Magical Creature Guide* and she'd seen pictures of them. Dragons were friendly, although in Twinkleland they didn't leave their caves very often and they were rather too large to visit the main towns.

The Princess was sure the monstrous beast eating a tree was *not* a dragon.

"It doesn't even have wings!" she pointed out.

"It looks more like a...dinosaur? But that would be impossible. Everyone knows they are extinct!"

The beastly *thing* seemed to have heard them and was headed their way.

"Yikes!" yelled Princess Pea. "We should probably hide!"

They all dived behind a large boulder and watched the immense and noisy creature as it passed by, crushing vegetation, petrifying the daisies and uprooting conifers to use as toothpicks.

But, after a few moments, the monstrous beast had trampled off, headed in the direction of Twinkletown.

"I think it's gone," said Princess Pea, her
heart thumping in her chest.

Unipiggle gave a reassuring grunt.

"Are y-y-you sure?" asked Arthur, trembling like jelly.

Just then, a shadow fell over them.

"Argggggh! Another **MONSTER**!" Arthur pulled his hat down over his eyes and desperately tried to make himself even smaller than he already was.

"I'm a **DRAGON**, you silly fool!" sighed a golden dragon, landing gracefully in front of them. "My name is Goldie!" The dragon bowed to the Princess and Unipiggle.

Princess Pea grinned with delight. "You ARE a dragon!" Meeting a dragon was one of her ambitions. "I'm Princess Pea, this is Unipiggle and that's Arthur the pixie."

"Did you happen to see…erm…a rather

large *dinosaur* pass this way?" asked Goldie casually.

"You mean to say that monstrous beast really *was* a dinosaur? Whatever next? Pigs might fly!" jabbered Arthur.

Unipiggle looked at the dragon suspiciously.

The dragon gulped. She'd not seen a unicorn pig before, but this one seemed rather shrewd.

Unipiggle nudged the Princess with his snout.

"Ah…" the Princess said. "How did *you* know it was a dinosaur?" she asked the dragon.

"Hmm, well, that is a good question." Goldie furrowed her scaly brow. She looked around guiltily, then lowered her voice and said softly, "I magicked it."

"You magicked a dinosaur?" Arthur squeaked.

"Yes, well, obviously I didn't *mean* to…" protested the dragon. "I *know* magic is banned… but there are so many regulations for us dragons to follow in Twinkleland."

"I mean, I haven't left Dragonton for forty-five-and-a-half moon cycles because…I don't like to GET IN THE WAY!"

"It's okay," Princess Pea said soothingly as Goldie hid her head under her wing. "But I still don't understand. Please can you explain *how* you magicked the dinosaur?"

"Well, that's the problem," Goldie cried. "I have no idea how I did it. I was just admiring my fossil collection, you see — one moment I was blowing the dust off a large dinosaur bone, and the next… **Zap! Boom!** A real-life dinosaur appeared."

"Just like that?" asked Princess Pea in awe.

"Just like that!" said Goldie. "I'm as shocked as you are. I've never practised any magic before. Unfortunately," the dragon continued, "it crashed out through my cave door and ran away."

"Hmm. Mummy and Daddy will be mad if the dinosaur goes near the palace," Princess Pea thought aloud. "Mummy hates mess and trouble and anything that breaks the rules. And Daddy doesn't like noise when he's practising the ukulele."

Goldie looked horrified. "I must try to stop it!"

Princess Pea turned to Unipiggle and Arthur. "Well, we wanted an adventure and it seems we've found one."

Unipiggle nodded bravely — he was ready for anything.

Arthur said nothing, but his expression was one of pure terror.

"We will help stop the dinosaur!" declared
Princess Pea.

"That is awfully kind of you," gushed the
dragon.

Princess Pea looked determined.

Unipiggle stomped his trotter.

Come on, everyone,
we need to think of
a plan. And fast!

7

Dinosaur Havoc!

The dinosaur stomped into Twinkletown.

SMASH!

CRASH!

BASH!

This dinosaur should have been called a **Donotmesswithmeasaurus**, because it was hungry, clumsy, grumpy and **RUDE!**

It **SMASHED** its dinosaur fists into the rooftops of Twinkletown's houses, gobbled up Baker Troll's cakes and even swallowed his fluffy pet cat (then spat it straight back out again like a soggy furball).

The dinosaur drank all the water from the mermaid fountain and **CRASHED** through the town, its long tail **BASHING** around behind it, taking out rows of tiny fairy cottages.

Then the dinosaur managed to destroy the library clock tower and knock off most of the roof tiles. The furious librarian wizard ran out and shook his crusty old wand, but nothing except useless sparks flew out. (This was also when he slipped on the *Unipiggy* poop — not that it mattered by then.)

The dinosaur's stompy feet shook the ground so much that cracks began to open up along the polished streets. It munched on the neatly trimmed hedges, the perfectly pruned trees, the immaculate lawns. There were giant footprints all over the place. It was mayhem! Everyone in Twinkletown ran for the safety of Twinkleland Palace, high on the hill.

Meanwhile, blissfully unaware of the terrible situation unfolding outside, King Barry was teaching a group of Palace Pixies to dance along to a terrible tune he was playing on the ukulele.

Queen Bee was busy instructing a Window Pixie to clean a very intricate stained-glass window in the shape of a flamingo. She gazed at the sparkling glass and suddenly thought to herself, *Princess Pea has been at the library a long time, I should send the King to Twinkletown to fetch her.*

Just then, the floors and walls of the palace began to rattle and shake. They shook so hard that the Queen knew it wasn't just her daughter and Unipiggle jumping on the beds upstairs this time. The flamingo window shattered into thousands of tiny pink shards!

Outside, the good folk of Twinkletown reached the palace gates in a big flock.

The Gate Pixie was overwhelmed. He unlocked the gates and directed the panicking hordes towards the front door of the palace.

HELP US!

Queen Bee marched upstairs to the Royal Balcony, where she could see all the way across Twinkleland. "What on **EARTH** is happening?!"

The dinosaur had got bored of Twinkletown and had set its sights on the nice shiny building with lots of pointy bits on top of the hill.

ROAR!

King Barry rushed to her side. "Are we having a party, dear? The hall is full of townsfolk! Goodness me, that's one angry...dragon!"

"I don't think it's a dragon," said the Queen. She'd met a few of them in the past and remembered them as rather shy and retiring creatures. But whatever this was, it wasn't welcome.

The ground was still shaking and Queen Bee was feeling quite unsteady. She gripped the balcony rail, while King Barry beat a hasty retreat.

The dinosaur had arrived at the gates.

The Gate Pixie fainted.

The beast ripped the sparkling gates out of the ground and jumped on them, crushing them with its enormous toes.

For a moment there was a pause as the dinosaur eyed the beautiful palace gardens... Then it grinned and rushed in. **SMASH! BASH! CRASH!** went the dinosaur.

(It was a good thing that Arthur wasn't there to see his lovely lawns being trampled on.)

Queen Bee was gobsmacked. *HOW VERY DARE IT!* She had never felt so **FURIOUS**. The monstrous beast was **RUINING** everything.

The dinosaur wasn't used to being bossed around, so it stopped, stared at the angry frilly person wearing a crown and...**LAUGHED**! A great big, stinky-dino-breath belly laugh.

HA
HO
HA!

The frilly person got angrier.
The dinosaur licked its lips.
Then the dinosaur lumbered
towards the Queen's balcony.

Saving the Royal Bacon

Inside the palace, King Barry was trying to calm everyone down. (Though he was secretly annoyed that his ukulele practice had been rudely interrupted.) But as he pondered how to help the Queen with this beastly problem, another horrifying thought filled the King's mind. Where was his daughter? She wasn't in the hall. Had she already been…? **GULP!**

"If anyone has any ideas on how to magic the wild creature away, that would be super!" the King announced feebly to the townsfolk.

There was a great deal of muttering.

"May I remind you, Your Highness, we're not allowed to use magic," piped up the Trumpet Pixie.

"But this is a big and terrible emergency!" croaked the King, who now had a headache.

"I'm not sure I can actually use my magic any more!" admitted one fairy.

"I'm very rusty," agreed the librarian wizard.

"Diamond Glitter's horn hasn't worked properly for ages," moaned a unicorn's groom. "All it does now is look pretty."

"You see, if you don't practise magic, you kind of forget," squeaked the forlorn Window-Cleaning Pixie.

The King shook his head in disbelief. Here he was, leader of a magical kingdom (though he didn't have any magic himself), with a dangerous dragon-or-whatever-it-was rampaging around, and not one of his subjects with magical powers could do *anything* about it? Maybe the *No Magic* rule was one rule too many...

Suddenly the King heard a very loud

EEEEEKKKkkk!

It was the Queen.

He rushed up to the hole where the window had been, just in time to see Queen Bee snatched from the balcony by the very smashy, bashy dinosaur.

But at that very moment, Princess Pea swooped into view.

She was alive! And she was in the sky!

The Princess was flying on the back of a large, gold and friendly-looking dragon. Around the dragon's tummy was a rope, and dangling on the end of that rope was the **Royal Unicorn pig**.

PUT me down this instant!

The King's eyebrows wiggled and danced
with amazement as he watched his daughter
zoom towards the palace — he'd never been so
pleased to see her.

As Goldie flew closer to the palace, Princess
Pea saw at once that her mummy might become
dinosaur dinner if she didn't act fast.

The Princess glanced down at the wonderful
Unipiggle, who was about to be used as bait.
Unipiggle winked back. He was the bravest
unicorn pig alive.

"Go on then!" hissed Goldie.

The Princess took a deep breath... "Here,
dino! Over here, dino!" called Princess Pea.
"How about a piggy for tea?!"

The dinosaur looked up at the funny

collection of a princess, a dragon and a unicorn pig in the sky. Then it snorted and turned its attention back to trying to eat the Queen, but her silly frilly wrapper tasted disgusting.

"You're ruining my favourite sea-silk gown!" the Queen shrieked.

"You need to try again!" the dragon urged Princess Pea.

"*Right, listen up, dinosaur!*" shouted the Princess as loudly as she could. She shimmied down the rope like it was her super-slidey pole, until she was standing on Unipiggle's back. "*You don't want to eat that nasty, frilly, chewy queen, you want to eat this soft and tender, juicy piggy-wig.*"

"Squeal! Squeal! Oink!" squealed Unipiggle,

spinning round on the end of his dangly rope under the dragon and wiggling his porky legs, as if to say, *Here I am, all ready to be eaten up!* He really was an heroic Unipiggle.

The dinosaur fixed his gaze upon poor Unipiggle.

The Princess gulped.

Dropping the unharmed Queen Bee in her half-chewed dress back onto the balcony, the dinosaur lurched towards Unipiggle.

Goldie flew in circles and Unipiggle spun around, grunting, just above the snapping jaws of the dinosaur below.

Princess Pea gritted her teeth and cried, "This is adventurous enough for me! It's time to lure the dinosaur far, far away from the palace... Go, Goldie, go! Bye, Mummy, bye, Daddy! I'll be back for tea, I promise!"

The Magical Lake

The dragon swooped down the hill, then flew
haphazardly over the broken roofs of
Twinkletown. Unipiggle and Princess Pea were
still spinning wildly on the end of the rope,
getting very dizzy. The dinosaur was in
hot pursuit.

"Hang on in there, Unipiggle!" Princess
Pea called out, clinging on for dear life
herself. *Perhaps this part of the plan wasn't
such a great idea,* the Princess thought…
but it was too late now.

"You're both very heavy," complained Goldie. "I really can't fly as fast or as high as I hoped."

Squeee! Squee!

Unipiggle shut his eyes tight as the dinosaur advanced on them.

"Dinosaur at ten paces!" the Princess yelled up to the dragon. Unipiggle wiggled and squirmed. Princess Pea tried to comfort him, but they could both smell nasty lizard-breath behind them.

"Dinosaur at five paces!"

Goldie turned her head and desperately tried to breathe fire at the dinosaur, but only managed to spit out a tiny flame — hardly enough to toast a marshmallow...

"Try flapping as hard as you can!" the Princess encouraged the dragon desperately.

With all her strength, Goldie
managed to lift them higher into
the air, just out of reach of the
dinosaur's drooling mouth.

But it wasn't over yet!

The dragon, the Princess and Unipiggle rocketed over the lush forest. They were a safer distance away from the rampaging beast now, though the dinosaur still **bashed, smashed** and **crashed** through the trees below.

Princess Pea fished out her notebook. It was hard to read directions with the pages flapping in the wind.

"Remember the plan, Goldie. Head towards the magical lake in the volcano! Hopefully that dinosaur is so heavy that it will sink into the mud of the boggy swamp and get well and truly stuck!" She turned to the map she had made.

"I think we're almost there — I do hope Arthur has found it alright."

As the Princess looked down, a dazzling, crystal-clear lake came into sight. The surface reflected rays of sunlight, and rainbows bounced off it like dolphins.

"That must be it!" said Goldie hopefully.

Unipiggle grunted — he was ready to ditch the dino!

They were relieved to
see that Arthur *had*
arrived, and he'd
even mowed an
area nearby to
create a makeshift
runway. He was
standing at the
end, frantically
waving his hat.

The dragon found
landing tricky.
She dived, she wobbled,
she lurched and tumbled… Unipiggle shot out
behind her on his rope, with Princess Pea still on
his back, and they all landed in a crumpled heap.

Arthur rushed to help the Princess to her feet, and they both untied Unipiggle from his rope.

Goldie lay there on her back, puffing and huffing, even though there was no time to rest.

The ground began to shake and the lake rippled.

"Here it comes!" wheezed the dragon.

"But WHERE is the boggy swamp?" cried Princess Pea. "The bog was definitely marked on the old map!" She looked around frantically, but could only see a beautiful lake surrounded by mossy green grassland and trees.

"Our plan involved mud and there's no mud here!" she cried. "It must have dried up! If we can't trap the dinosaur in the mud, how can we stop it?"

Unipiggle, Arthur and Goldie looked at each other. They had no idea.

Princess Pea thought fast. "Didn't Sir Sneeze-A-Lot say the lake grants magical wishes?

Unipiggle, dip your horn in and wish for the lake to turn swampy!"

Unipiggle was still a little dizzy from all the swinging around and being piggy-bait, but he got up and ran to the edge of the lake, oinking bravely. He bent his head and dipped his horn into the water.

"Bravo, Unipiggle," called Goldie admiringly.

Smash! Bash! Crash!

The dinosaur appeared on the other side of the lake.

"Is anything happening?" Arthur asked Unipiggle anxiously.

The lake shimmered as Unipiggle's horn glowed with magic.

He stepped back as the water swirled and sloshed and gurgled.

Princess Pea held her breath.

Arthur held his ears.

Goldie nervously puffed out little smoke rings…

Had Unipiggle magicked a boggy swamp?

Unipiggle leaned forward and slurped a mouthful of muddy water — except it wasn't mud at all…

Unipiggle had accidentally turned the water into **chocolate**!

The Princess was disappointed. The lake wasn't magical after all. That old Sir Sneeze-A-Lot had got *everything* wrong and now the dinosaur would probably eat them all. Goldie was too tired to go any further.

It was then that something amazing happened. Maybe the lake really *was* magical after all, or maybe the old volcano underneath it had been stirred into life by all the commotion. Whatever the reason, things started to heat up just at the right moment.

The chocolate lake began to bubble…

RUMBLE RUMBLE!

First the delicious smell of warming chocolate filled the air, then fountains of chocolate shot out of the lake in big bubbly explosions. The lake started to flood and a waterfall of warm chocolate gushed straight towards the dinosaur.

There was no escape.

Huh?

Caught in the flow, the dinosaur was completely coated in sticky chocolate, which cooled so quickly the dino couldn't even move a talon. It was well and truly trapped.

"Well, that stopped it," giggled Princess Pea with relief, jumping up and down with Unipiggle.

But a chocolate dinosaur? Yuck! I'd rather eat a chocolate sprout!

"Well Done" Stickers

So it was that Princess Pea arrived back just in time for tea (as promised) with the brave Unipiggle and the helpful Arthur at her side. She also brought the reluctant Goldie along to introduce to her parents.

The King and Queen were so happy to see their daughter home in one piece that they hardly noticed that Princess Pea had ripped her royal cape or had been paddling in chocolate and they didn't ask how many marshmallows she'd eaten that day.

They even nodded sympathetically when Goldie admitted the **smashy-bashy-crashy** dinosaur was the result of a magical accident.

As the unlikely heroes finished their story, the townsfolk in the Grand Hall erupted into applause. Even the unicorns neighed joyously as Unipiggle demonstrated how he had saved the day. The Awards Pixie awarded each of the adventurers a royal *Well Done* sticker for saving the kingdom. Princess Pea had never been given a *Well Done* sticker before.

The Queen nodded to the Announcement Pixie to speak on her behalf.

Those in Twinkletown who no longer have a roof can stay in the palace until they do!

The King stood up. "And as a treat, the Queen and I have decided we shall host a little party tomorrow. We'll invite everyone in Twinkleland to it — even the dragons, as long as they're careful."

Everyone gasped in appreciation.

"It will be a special **TIDY-UP** party!" added the Queen, as if it was the best idea she'd ever had.

Princess Pea groaned and Unipiggle rolled his eyes, but they soon cheered up when Baker Troll offered to bake a celebratory volcano-lake cake for the occasion.

The Princess and Unipiggle finished eating their tea while the Palace Pixies started plumping up fluffy white pillows and handing out sleeping bags to the guests. Goldie the dragon decided a big sleepover wasn't for her, so she made herself comfortable on the Second Best Palace lawn.

Arthur helpfully found her a broom she could
use as a toothbrush.

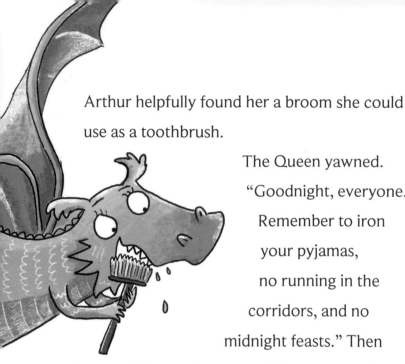

The Queen yawned.
"Goodnight, everyone.
Remember to iron
your pyjamas,
no running in the
corridors, and no
midnight feasts." Then
she gave Princess Pea a grateful squeeze before
retiring to her royal chamber.

Princess Pea was just thinking that she might
have enough energy to pile up the spare pillows
to create a makeshift bouncy castle, when the
King decided to play his captive audience a
newly composed song...

"I call this one 'Chocolate Lava'!"

Oh no! Princess Pea nudged Unipiggle. Perhaps it *was* time for them to go to bed.

"Goodnight, Unipiggle! Goodnight, Princess Pea!" everyone cheered.

Princess Pea left the hall glowing with pride. Their adventure had been scary but fun! As they snuggled under the covers, Princess Pea took out her notebook with the map. There were so many new places to explore! Unipiggle oinked happily.

They couldn't wait to have more adventures together.

Hey, wait a minute!
What happened to the
chocolate dinosaur?

After a day or so, the dinosaur discovered that the brown sticky stuff it was covered in was edible and…delicious! With delight, the dino ate itself free. The chocolate was so sweet and yummy that the dinosaur became vegetarian and now lives happily (and quietly), grazing on the bountiful sweet trees that grow around the chocolate volcano lake.

HOW TO DRAW A DRAGON

You will need: a pencil, a black pen, a rubber and colouring pencils

Step 1: Use a pencil to draw one small square and two ovals like this...

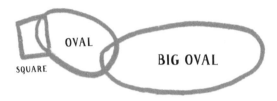

OVAL

SQUARE

BIG OVAL

Step 2: Add shapes for the ears, wings, arms, legs and tail.

TWO WINGS

TWO TRIANGLES
FOR EARS

TWO LINES AND
A TRIANGLE FOR
ITS TAIL

ARMS

LEGS

Step 3: Draw your dragon on top of the pencil shapes in pen.

COPY THESE WINGS

ADD EYES, NOSTRILS
AND A MOUTH

DRAW LOTS OF SCALES
ALONG ITS HEAD, BACK
AND TAIL.

Step 4: Wait for the ink to dry, then rub out all the pencil lines.

Step 5: Use your colouring pencils to colour in the dragon. Hooray!

A LOUD, MUDDY and PROUD UNIPIGGLE quiz!

1) Princess Pea lives in which palace?

2) Unipiggle can turn objects into which delicious food?

3) Are you allowed to use magic in Twinkleland?

4) What colour is Unipiggle's poop?

5) Which instrument does King Barry like to play?

6) What is the name of the Gardener Pixie who accompanies Unipiggle and Princess Pea on their adventure?

7) Are unicorns snooty and vain or lovely and kind?

8) Does Princess Pea want to have adventures and explore Twinkleland, or stay in the palace and eat green porridge?

ANSWERS

1) Twinkleland Palace

2) Chocolate

3) No! (Except in a big and terrible emergency.)

4) Rainbow-coloured!

5) The ukelele

6) Arthur

7) Snooty and vain

8) Have adventures and explore Twinkleland!

For more UNIPIGGLE activities, trot to:
www.unipiggle.com

HANNAH SHAW

Hannah Shaw *is a multi-award-winning author and illustrator. When she was little she wanted to be a gymnast or a champion rollerskater or a penguin keeper but instead she picked up a pen and began to draw.*

Hannah now lives in Gloucestershire with her messy family. One day she hopes to meet a magical pig, but until then, she's very happy bringing UNIPIGGLE to life with her words and pictures.

Find out more about Hannah Shaw at
www.hannahshawillustrator.co.uk